# TAM LIN

An old ballad retold by JANE YOLEN

and illustrated by CHARLES MIKOLAYCAK

# TAM LIN

Harcourt Brace Jovanovich, Publishers

San Diego   New York   London

HBJ

Text copyright © 1990 by Jane Yolen
Illustrations copyright © 1990 by Charles Mikolaycak

All rights reserved. No part of this publication
may be reproduced or transmitted in any form or
by any means, electronic or mechanical, including
photocopy, recording, or any information storage
and retrieval system, without permission in
writing from the publisher.

Requests for permission to make copies of
any part of the work should be mailed to:
Permissions Department,
Harcourt Brace Jovanovich, Publishers,
Orlando, Florida 32887.

Library of Congress Cataloging-in-Publication Data
Yolen, Jane.
Tam Lin.
Summary: In this retelling of an old Scottish ballad,
a Scottish lass, on the Halloween after her sixteenth
birthday, reclaims her family home which has been held
for years by the fairies and at the same time effects the
release of Tam Lin, a human held captive by the Queen
of the Fey.
[1. Fairy tales. 2. Folklore—Scotland]
I. Mikolaycak, Charles, ill. II. Title.
PZ8.Y78Tam   1990     [398.2]     88-2280
ISBN 0-15-284261-6

First edition   A B C D E

The illustrations in this book were done in
watercolor and colored pencil on Diazo prints.
The display type was handlettered by Judythe Sieck.
The text type was set via the linotron in Fournier
by Thompson Type, San Diego, California.
Printed and bound by Tien Wah Press, Singapore
Production supervision by Warren Wallerstein
and Ginger Boyer
Designed by Charles Mikolaycak and Joy Chu

For the balladeers in my life:
Will Yolen, who taught me cowboy songs,
Steven Yolen, who sang blues & bluegrass with me,
Burt & Honey Knopp and all their hootenannies,
Mike Lieber, my college singing partner,
and my son Adam Stemple, who writes his own.

—*J. Y.*

To all who showed concern and love,
especially Carole.

—*C. M.*

There was once a strange, forbidding castle with ruined towers on a weedy piece of land called Carterhaugh. Many years had passed since humans lived there. It had been the most beautiful home in the land. Now all the children were warned against it.

"Do not go down to Carterhaugh," said their mothers and nurses. "There is an awful smell to the place. There are prickers and briars, thistles and thorns."

"Do not go down to Carterhaugh," said their fathers and tutors. "There are terrible shadows and odd, harsh cries in the undergrowth. Oh, do not go down to Carterhaugh."

The younger children listened to the warnings. But some of the older boys went secretly on dares, leaving tokens of their passing—garlands or rings, and once a fine green mantle.

There *was* an awful smell to the place, like apples gone bad, or dead mice in the walls, or dirty water in an unused well. And there *were* moving shadows where no shadows should be.

Those few who went to visit Carterhaugh did not stay long, and they had bad dreams for many nights after.

Now there was one girl, Jennet MacKenzie, who had skin the color of new cream and hair the red-gold of a sunrise. And Jennet laughed at them all.

"Are you brave boys afraid of shadows and smells?" she asked. "*I* am not afraid. Besides, my father's father's father owned Carterhaugh. It should be mine by right, though I am not allowed to claim it. MacKenzies should rule that land, and MacKenzie voices should fill the halls of that castle. When I am old enough, claim it I will!"

Her mother cautioned her to be silent, and her father wept openly when she said she would go. They loved their only child dearly, and they were truly afraid for her.

"Our home is in the village now," they said. "And that is good enough for us."

But Jennet always had a mind of her own, even as a wee girl. The villagers all said she would never marry, no matter that her father was chief of the clan. No man would want her, even for all her beauty and her father's name. For she always spoke what she thought. And *what* she thought was never quite proper for a fine young lady.

"I will go," Jennet said, "for I am not afraid. I will go when I am old enough to win back Carterhaugh for our clan."

On the day she turned sixteen, the day she came into her inheritance, Jennet twisted her long, red-gold hair into a braid and pinned it to the top of her head. She put on her brand-new birthday gown, as green as young willow. She fastened the MacKenzie plaid across her shoulder and secured it with a golden brooch. Then she went down the stairs to greet her guests. She laughed and danced, as if this birthday were like any other. But though she fooled her friends, she could not fool her parents.

"Do not go down to Carterhaugh," they begged her. Her father nervously turned the great ruby ring on his finger, and her mother crushed a pale rosebud in her hand. "That land no longer belongs to the MacKenzies, girl. It belongs to the Fair Folk now, the Faeries, the Fey. Nothing lives there but ghosts and boggles and wicked things. Do not go, Jennet. *Do not go.*"

But as soon as the party was over and the last of the guests' horses had gone down the long, winding road, Jennet pulled the plaid up over her hair. She put on her walking shoes, tucked her skirts above her knees, and bounded up and over the heathery hills toward the tumbledown towers of Carterhaugh.

By the time she was close enough to see the walls, the sun was at the level of the hilltops. And by the time she was standing by the broken door, the sun was behind the hills. Night birds called mournfully from the nearest trees. The shadows of briars seemed sharper than the briars themselves. The only spot of color, besides Jennet's green gown and plaid and her red-gold hair, was on a bush growing by the ruined door. A single rose bloomed there, the color of spilled blood.

Jennet *was* afraid, but she would not show it. In a voice that was strong, though the echo of it trembled, she called out: "Today I have come into my inheritance. Today, by law, I can claim what is my own. This house and this land belonged to my father's father's father and was stolen from him by the Fey. Its great beauty has been destroyed. So I take this rose, the only thing of beauty left here, as my pledge. I shall take back Carterhaugh from the Fey and restore it to humankind."

She bent over and plucked the rose, heedless of the pricking thorns.

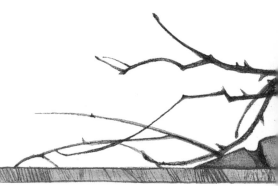

But as the rose stalk bent and broke, a great wind suddenly blew across the clearing, whistling over the broken stones. A single flash of lightning lit the evening sky. Standing in front of her, where a moment before no one had been, was a young man dressed in velvet and kilt. He was as handsome as a prince of the Fey.

"Who is it who pulls the rose and calls me back to the world of men?" His voice was hollow-sounding, as if it came from far away.

Startled, Jennet could not answer.

The young man spoke again, his voice sounding fuller this time. "Who calls me from the land of the Ever-Fair?"

At that, Jennet recovered her wits and laughed. "There is no land of the Ever-Fair, no country of the Fey. It is but a nursery tale. We live in this world, side by side, and the Fey are thieves. We all grow old in time."

The young man sighed. "I, too, once believed that. But as I was riding on a summer's eve near the house of my father's friend, the Laird MacKenzie, my horse shied, and I fell off. I must have hit my head, for I lay in a faint upon the hillside.

"The Queen of the Fey found me and took me inside the green hill. I have lived there ever since. Believe me, in the land of the Fey there is no old age. And there is no natural death." He stopped abruptly.

"How long is 'ever since'?" Jennet asked. "You do not look older than I, and I am sixteen today."

"Alas, child, I am ten times sixteen, older than the oldest man alive outside the hill."

Jennet smiled. "That cannot be. Your face is young, your limbs are strong, and you are fair. What is your name?"

"I am called Tam Lin," he said.

"Tam Lin! But that was the name of a boy who disappeared when my father's father's father was still alive," Jennet said.

He nodded. "When I rode off that summer's day, this house

stood upright and unbroken." He gestured to the ruins.

Jennet went over to him and put the rose in his hand. "Well, Tam Lin, that house shall stand upright and tall again, for my name is Jennet MacKenzie, and the house is rightfully mine."

Tam Lin laughed, but it was a rusty sound, as if he had not laughed for a long time. "That I should like to see," he said, kissing her hand.

"I promise you shall."

But Tam Lin's face grew long and sad. "After this Hallow's Eve, I shall see nothing ever again." His hand still held hers, but his fingers had grown cold as snow.

"This Saturday night?" Jennet asked. "But why? Are you ill? Or have you done something wicked for which you must hang?"

"Neither and both, Jennet. This Halloween, as on all solstice nights, the human world and the faery world sit side by side. The moonlight is the only door between them. Through that door the Fey can cross at will. Over the moors, past Selkirk town, down to Miles Cross where the holy well stands, the Fey shall ride this Hallow's Eve, and I shall ride with them as I have done every seven years since the day they stole me away." He shivered and took his hand from hers.

She wondered that she missed that hand, so cold and strong in hers. "What is wrong with that riding?"

He stared at the sky. The moon stood high above them, and his face was cast in silver, like a mask in a mummer's play. "Every seven years, Jennet, the Fey kill one of their human captives. It is their tithe to Hell. For seven years times seven years and seven years again, I have not been the chosen one, for the queen has loved me well. But now she loves another, and this Hallow's Eve *I* am to be the sacrifice."

Jennet felt her heart stop. Tears started in her eyes. "Can you run, Tam Lin?"

"I cannot."

"Can no one save you?"

"None."

"No one at all?"

"Only my own true human love," he said. "But alas, all who love me are long dead, and the grass is growing over their graves."

"Then I shall save you!" Jennet cried. "Or die as I try. If no one else in this human world loves you, then I must."

Tam Lin took her in his arms and told her what she must do. His words were like his kisses—cold, distant, and fierce.

On Hallow's Eve Jennet stole away from her house. She wore a skirt
and bodice as red as human blood. Over her head and shoulders
she wore a mantle as green as grass so that the Fey might not see
her, for green was the Fey's own color. In her left pocket she
carried earth from her garden at home, and in her right, a bottle of
holy water she had begged from the priest. All this Tam Lin had
told her to bring.

　　She crept over the hills to Miles Cross and shivered as she
crouched by the well. In the dark her hair was no longer like

sunrise but the color of dusk, after the sun has set. All about her was a great white mist, and she could see nothing beyond the crossroads, not the path, nor the trees on either side, nor the canopy of sky.

A long, long time she waited, afraid to move. And then the great bell in the Selkirk tower tolled twelve. When the last low note had faded away, Jennet heard an answering ring from way down the road, high and jangling.

Turning toward the sound, she waited as the white moonlit mist parted, like a huge door opening, and through it rode the faery troop. The bells on the horses' harnesses rang out with every step, and all about them was an unearthly light.

Jennet remembered Tam Lin's instructions, and she let the first horse pass her by. It was black as coal, black as the pit's bottom, black as death. On its back was a human man as tall and fair as a prince, but his face was long, and he did not smile.

Then Jennet made ready to stand, but she recalled what Tam Lin had told her, and she let the second horse go by as well. It was as brown as oakwood, brown as old blood, brown as earth in a grave. On its back was a human man as tall and as fair as a king, but his face, too, was long, and he did not smile.

Then before she could stand, the third horse came by. It was white as snow, white as the froth on the waves, white as the milk on the mouth of a babe. On this horse sat a human man who was as tall and as fair as a saint. And though his face was long, around his mouth played a ghost of a smile.

"Tam Lin!" Jennet cried out. She leaped from her place behind the well, ran over to the white horse, pulled down the rider, and held him fast in her arms.

In an instant the faery troop surrounded them. The horses were bridled in gold and shod in silver, and on each one's head shone a bright jewel. The riders of the Fey were all tall and stern, but the tallest and the sternest was the Faery Queen. Her dress was of green, all the greens of the forest, and her white hair hung in a hundred braids down her back.

"Give me Tam Lin," cried the Faery Queen, "and I shall give you all the gold and silver you see here."

Jennet shook her head. "I have enough gold in my mother's hair and silver in my father's," she said. "I need none of yours."

"Give me Tam Lin," cried the queen, "and I shall give you the jewels on my horses' heads."

Jennet smiled. "The only jewels I need shine in my true love's eyes."

The queen stared at Jennet, as if reading her soul. Then she cried out, "Give me my Tam Lin, and I shall return to you your Carterhaugh."

For a moment—only a moment—Jennet was silent with thought. Her mind filled with the beauty of the house, not as it would be but as it once had been. Then she shook her head to cast off the queen's enchantment, and laughed.

"I shall have Carterhaugh whether you will it or not, O Queen. Whatever you do, I shall hold tight to both Tam Lin and Carterhaugh."

The queen rose up in her stirrups, and her face was grim. She pointed her hand at Jennet, and a great cold light poured from her fingertips. *"You do not hold Tam Lin even now!"* she cried.

With a great wrenching twist, Tam Lin almost tore from Jennet's arms. And when she looked at him, he had turned into a hideous serpent with lidless eyes and thousands of gray-green scales.

But Jennet held on, though she closed her eyes at the sight.

The Faery Queen spoke again. "What do you hold now, Jennet?"

The long serpent twisted around her. She felt a hot breath on her face and sharp claws at her breast. When she opened her eyes there was a lion's head behind her, its teeth bared.

But still Jennet held on.

"And what do you hold now, human girl?" asked the queen.

The lion shrank, its golden mane flaring into tendrils of flame. Its warm body grew fiery hot. Now she held a burning brand, but still she would not let go.

Heedless of the fire that seared her, Jennet ran to the well, and at the last moment, she threw the brand in. Then she took the bottle of holy water from her pocket and sprinkled it over the well and herself.

At once the fire went out, and Tam Lin climbed from the well. His faery clothing had been burned away, so he stood in nothing but his human skin.

Jennet threw her mantle over him and turned toward the queen.

"The earth," Tam Lin whispered urgently. "Do not forget the earth."

Then Jennet remembered. She put her hand to her pocket and drew out the brown garden earth, sprinkling it in a great circle around them, a circle of protection against the power of the Fey.

"Done!" she whispered back.

Then, hand in hand, they faced the queen.

Curses on you, Jennet MacKenzie!" screamed the Faery Queen. "And curses on your hall. And as for you, Tam Lin, if I had forseen your treachery, I would have plucked out your human eyes and heart and given you ones of wood."

But Tam Lin laughed. "We stand here protected by a circle of earth, with holy water upon our heads. Your curses return from us to thee, O Queen of the Ever-Fair. And look!" He pointed to the horizon where the sun was just dawning. "Your power is over. Be gone."

The queen and her troop turned back through the mist and rode silently away over the moonlight like so many shadows. Though Jennet listened for a long, long time, she heard no more faery bells.

And so Jennet and Tam Lin were married. It is said in Selkirk that they lived a long and happy life together in the great stone castle Jennet restored and renamed Carter Hall. And that their children's children's children lived there happily ever after.

But whether this is true or not, who can say? Only those with pure hearts, ready laughs, and a memory of mist on a moonlit road know for sure. And as for them, they are long in their quiet, grassy graves.

# ABOUT TAM LIN

The ballad of "Tam Lin" is one of the most ancient and popular of the Scottish ballads. It is first mentioned in a ballad book of 1549, yet there are many versions still sung today throughout the Border country and in Aberdeenshire.

> O I forbid you, maidens a'
>> That wear gold in your hair,
> To come or go by Carterhaugh
>> For young Tam Lin is there.

Tam Lin or Tamlane or Tam-a-Lin, captive of the faeries or the Fair Folk, is summoned by the broken rose, a conventional way of calling the lord of a faery garden.

> "Why pulls thou the rose, Janet,
>> And why breaks thou the wand,
> And why comes thou to Carterhaugh
>> Withoutten my command?"

Every seven years, according to ancient stories, the elves had to sacrifice one of their own as a payment to Hell. Whenever they could, they substituted one of the abducted humans.

> "And pleasant is the fairy land,
>> But an eerie tale to tell,
> Ay at the end of seven years
>> We pay a tiend to hell;
> I am so fair and full of flesh,
>> I'm feared it be myself."

It is an old belief that the faery troop rides on horses bridled in gold and shod in silver. The enchantment of turning a human into different repulsive shapes is a motif that goes back to Greek mythology.

"And then I'll be your own true love,
I'll turn a naked knight;
Then cover me with your green mantle,
And cover me out of sight."

There is a plain on the Yarrow near Selkirk called Carterhaugh where, according to an old manuscript, "they show two or three rings on the ground where the stands of milk and water for the fairies stood, and upon which grass never grows."

In most of the other old ballads, it is the man who does the rescuing. But in this one, it is Jennet (or Janet, or Margaret, depending upon which version one sings) who braves the wrath of the Faery Queen herself to win her own true love.

The MacKenzie clan exists, but not in the area of Carterhaugh. The tartans shown here were created by the artist for the story. After all, a faery tale demands its own colors and plaids.

Thanks to Sarah and Norbert.  —C.M.